For Peter and Laura,
and their prizewinning pup,
Huckleberry!
—A.S.C.

Biscuit Wins a Prize
Text copyright © 2004 by Alyssa Satin Capucilli
Illustrations copyright © 2004 by Pat Schories
Printed in the U.S.A. All rights reserved.
www.harperchildrens.com
Library of Congress Cataloging-in-Publication Data
Capucilli, Alyssa Satin   ,
Biscuit wins a prize / story by Alyssa Satin Capucilli; pictures by Pat Schories.
    p.   cm. — (My first I can read book)
Summary: Biscuit, a small puppy, gets excited when he is entered in a pet show.
ISBN 0-06-009455-9 — ISBN 0-06-009457-5 (lib. bdg.)
[1. Dogs—Fiction. 2. Pet shows—Fiction.] I. Schories, Pat, ill. II. Title. III. Series.
PZ7.C179Bitc 2004
[E]—dc21
2002154809

1 2 3 4 5 6 7 8 9 10 ❖ First Edition

MY FIRST
I Can Read Book®

Biscuit
Wins a Prize

story by ALYSSA SATIN CAPUCILLI
pictures by PAT SCHORIES

HarperCollins*Publishers*

Here, Biscuit.

It's time for the pet show!

Woof, woof!

There will be lots of pets,
and prizes, too!
Woof, woof!

Come along, sweet puppy.

You want to look your best.

Woof!

Hold still, Biscuit.

Woof, woof!

Funny puppy! Don't tug now!

Hold still, Biscuit.

Woof, woof!

Oh, Biscuit!

It's not time to roll over.

Woof, woof!

It's time for the pet show!

Look at all the pets, Biscuit.

Woof, woof!

Biscuit sees his friend Puddles.

Bow wow!

Woof, woof!

Biscuit sees his friend Sam.

Ruff!

Woof, woof!

13

Biscuit sees

lots of new friends, too.

Woof, woof!

Hold still now, Biscuit.

Here comes the judge.

16

Woof!

Oh no, Biscuit. Come back!

Biscuit wants
to see the fish.
Woof!

Biscuit wants
to see the bunnies.
Woof!

Woof, woof!

Biscuit wants
to see all of the pets
at the pet show!

Silly puppy! Here you are.

What prize will you win now?
Woof, woof!

Oh, Biscuit!

You won the best prize of all!

Woof!